Bam-Boo & I Wish

Early★Reader

First American edition published in 2019 by Lerner Publishing Group, Inc.

An original concept by Alice Hemming

Illustrated by Julia Seal

First published by Maverick Arts Publishing Limited

Maverick
arts publishing

Licensed Edition
Bam-Boo & I Wish

Lerner Publications Company
A division of Lerner Publishing Group, Inc.
241 First Avenue North
Minneapolis, MN 55401 USA

For reading levels and more information, look up this title at www.lernerbooks.com.

Main body text set in Mikado a. Typeface provided by HVD Fonts.

Library of Congress Cataloging-in-Publication Data

Names: Hemming, Alice, author. | Seal, Julia, illustrator.
Title: Bam-Boo & I wish / by Alice Hemming ; illustrated by Julia Seal.
Other titles: Bam-Boo and I wish
Description: First American edition. | Minneapolis : Lerner Publications, 2019. | Series: Early bird readers. Red (Early bird stories).
Identifiers: LCCN 2018017810 (print) | LCCN 2018025407 (ebook) | ISBN 9781541543171 (eb pdf) | ISBN 9781541541634 (lb : alk. paper) | ISBN 9781541546240 (pb : alk. paper)
Subjects: LCSH: Readers—Animals. | Readers (Primary) | Animals—Juvenile literature.
Classification: LCC PE1127.A6 (ebook) | LCC PE1127.A6 H46 2019 (print) | DDC 428.6/2—dc23

LC record available at https://lccn.loc.gov/2018017810

Manufactured in the United States of America
1-45337-38987-6/22/2018

Bam-Boo & I Wish

Alice Hemming

Illustrated by
Julia Seal

Lerner Publications ◆ Minneapolis

The Letter "B"

Trace the lowercase and uppercase letter with a finger. Sound out the letter.

Down,
up,
around

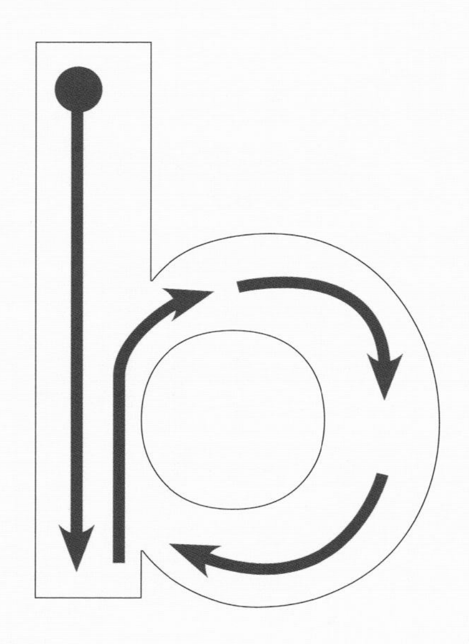

Down,
up,
around,
around

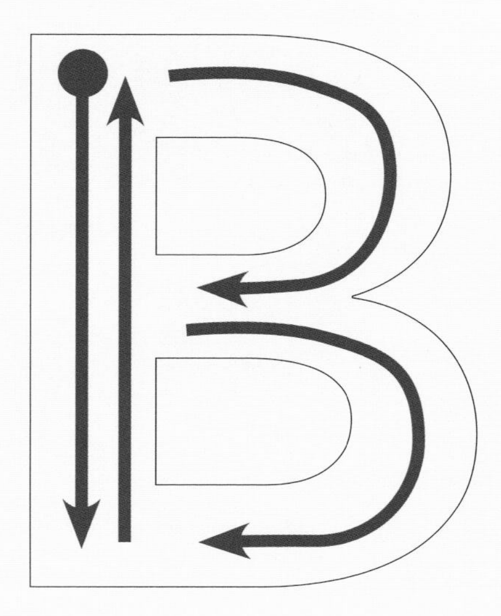

Some words to familiarize:

High-frequency words:

to be you the no it is off has

Tips for Reading *Bam-Boo*

- Practice the tricky words listed above before reading the story.

- If the reader struggles with any of the other words, ask them to look for sounds they know in the word. Encourage them to sound out the words and help them read the words if necessary.

- After reading the story, ask the reader the places that Bam did not hide and then ask where he did hide.

Fun Activity

Play a game of hide and seek.

Bam-Boo

Bam is a panda.

It is a lot of fun
to be a panda!

Bam has run off!

Can you spot Bam up in the tree?

No, that thing in the tree is a bird.

Can you spot Bam on the big rocks?

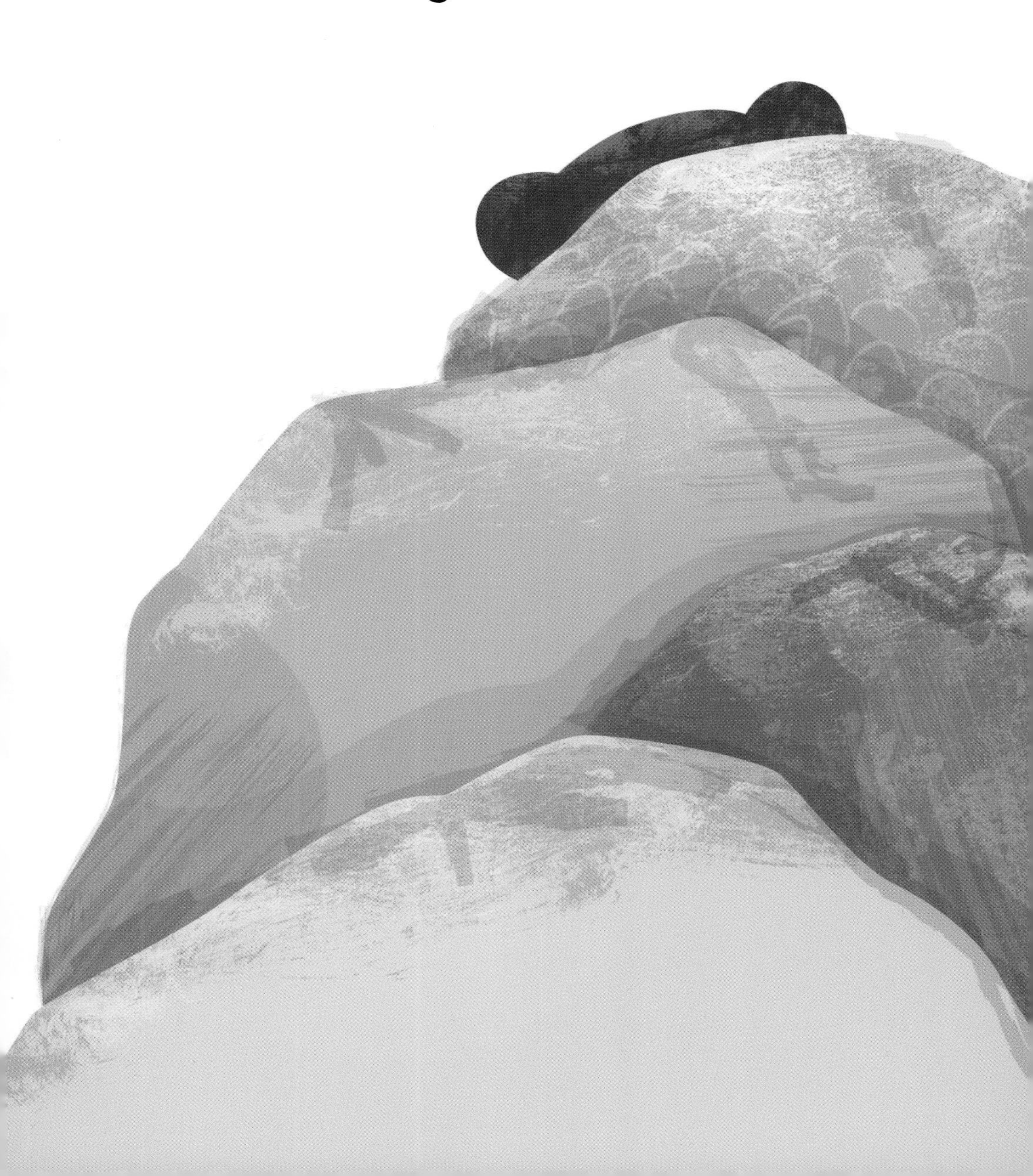

No, a frog is up on the rocks.

Ribbit.

Can you spot him in the bam . . .

Boo!

Bam is in the bamboo.

The Letter "W"

Trace the lowercase and uppercase letter with a finger. Sound out the letter.

Down,
up,
down,
up

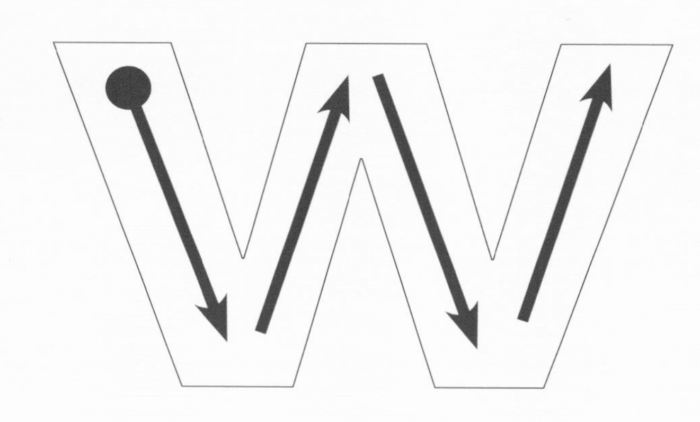

Some words to familiarize:

High-frequency words:

I the on a in to

Tips for Reading *I Wish*

- Practice the tricky words listed above before reading the story.

- If the reader struggles with any of the other words, ask them to look for sounds they know in the word. Encourage them to sound out the words and help them read the words if necessary.

- After reading the story, ask the reader if they remember what the different characters wished for.

Fun Activity

Ask the reader what they would wish for if they went to a magic wishing well.

I Wish

I am the Wishing Well on the hill.
Put a coin in the bucket.

Tell me your wish.

I wish for
a prince!

Put a coin in the bucket.
Tell me your wish.

We wish for . . .

A horse!

Put a coin in the bucket.
Tell me your wish.

I wish for . . .

Fun frogs
to hop with!

Leveled for Guided Reading

Early Bird Stories have been edited and leveled by leading educational consultants to correspond with guided reading levels. The levels are assigned by taking into account the content, language style, layout, and phonics used in each book.

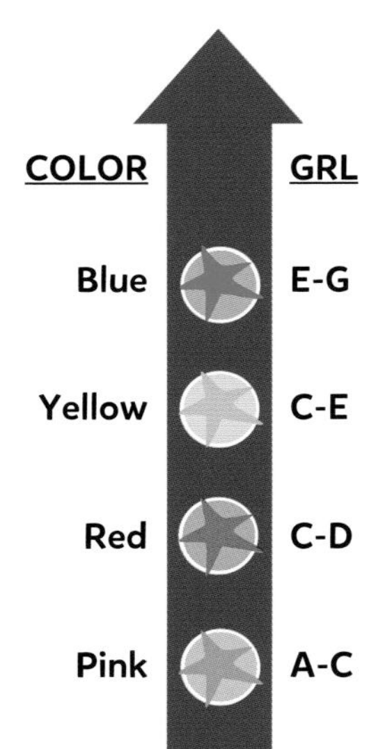